X

HANS CHRISTIAN ANDERSEN
The Snow Queen

Pictures by SUSAN JEFFERS

Retold by Amy Ehrlich

The Dial Press
New York

Published by
The Dial Press
1 Dag Hammarskjold Plaza
New York, New York 10017

Library of Congress Cataloging in Publication Data
Ehrlich, Amy, 1942– The Snow Queen.
Summary/The strength of a little girl's love enables her to overcome
many obstacles and free a boy from the Snow Queen's spell.
[1. Fairy tales] I. Jeffers, Susan, ill.
II. Andersen, H. C. (Hans Christian), 1805–1875. Sneedronningen.
III. Title.
PZ8.E32Sn [Fic] 82-70199
ISBN 0-8037-8011-7 AACR2
ISBN 0-8037-8029-X (lib. bdg.)

The full-color artwork was prepared using a fine-line pen with ink and dyes.
They were applied over a detailed pencil drawing that was then erased.
The artwork was camera-separated by Princeton Polychrome Press.
The book was printed by Holyoke Lithograph Co., Inc.,
and bound by A. Horowitz & Sons, Bookbinders.

For PJF with admiration and affection

Long, long ago when trolls still lived upon the earth, there was one more evil than all the others. He was called the devil. He loved to mock human beings, and so he invented a mirror that made everything that was beautiful and good appear strange and horrid.

At first the trolls only played with the mirror, holding it to the world and laughing at the reflections. But one day they flew up into the sky with it, and the mirror spun out of their hands. Down, down, down it fell, shattering into a million pieces. Some were as tiny as grains of sand, and when the wind came, it blew the pieces everywhere.

If one of these ever entered a person's eye, nothing looked right again. But far worse was the fate of someone whose heart was pierced by a sliver of the mirror. The person would soon forget the pain. He would go on as before, never knowing that the heart inside him had frozen into ice.

At a time when the tiniest fragments of the devil's mirror were still swirling through the air, a boy and a girl lived very near each other in a big city. The boy's name was Kai, and the girl's name was Gerda. They were good friends and loved nothing better than to play in the window gardens that leaned from the gables of their houses. In the summer they could sit under the rose trees and walk easily from one house to the other.

In the winter, when the windows were tightly closed and covered with ice, Gerda would run down the stairs and through the snowy yard to Kai's house. The two children heated copper coins upon the stove and pressed them to the

6

windows. A perfect small peephole was made in this way, and they could see across the wintry sky.

"The white bees are swarming," said the old Grandmother.

"Do they have a queen too?" asked Kai.

The Grandmother nodded. "She always stays in the center of the swarm. On snowy nights she flies through the streets of the town and looks in at the windows. Perhaps you have seen the ice patterns she leaves behind."

"Yes, I've seen them!" exclaimed Kai, and then he knew that what the Grandmother said was true.

Late that night, as Kai was getting ready for bed, he went to the window and looked out through his peephole. It was snowing softly. As Kai watched, the snowflakes piled one on the other until they took the shape of a woman. She was made of glittering ice. Her eyes shone like two stars, yet neither rest nor peace was in them. She nodded and beckoned to Kai. He jumped back in terror, and in that moment a shadow passed the window as if a great bird had flown by.

It was the last storm of winter. Soon the thaws came and the earth grew green. Once again roses bloomed in the window gardens, and the children were able to sit outside.

Late one afternoon as the church bells struck the hour, Kai suddenly cried out.

"What is it?" asked Gerda.

"Something pricked my heart," Kai said, and then he gasped again. "Something sharp is in my eye."

Gerda looked into Kai's eyes. There was nothing to be seen, but she cried because she felt sorry for him.

"I think it is gone now," said Kai. But he was wrong. For one splinter of the devil's mirror had entered his eye, and the other had pierced his heart. Instantly he turned on Gerda and began to mock her. "Why are you crying? You look ugly when you cry. There is nothing the matter with me.

"Look!" he shouted. "That rose up there is growing all crooked, and that one has been eaten by a worm. How horrid they are!" Then he tore off the roses and stamped on them.

"What are you doing, Kai?" cried Gerda. And when he saw how frightened she was, he pulled off another flower and climbed through the window into his own house, leaving Gerda to sit outside all alone.

No longer would he consent to play with her. Now his games were more grown-up. One winter day when snow was falling, he came by with his sled upon his back and wearing his woolen hat. He screamed into Gerda's ear as loudly as he could. "I have been allowed to go down to the square and play with the other boys!" And away he went without ever looking back.

Now it was the custom in that town for the bigger boys to tie their sleds onto the farmers' carts. They would travel fast over the hard, packed snow and get a wonderful ride. While they were playing in this way, a big white sled came into the square and circled it twice. Quickly Kai tied his little sled onto the big one. He wanted to show the older boys how daring he was.

Faster and faster they rode. Soon the town was far behind them. Kai wanted to untie his sled, but each time he was about to do it, the driver smiled at him so kindly that he didn't. It was as if they were already friends. The snow fell more thickly. Snowflakes swirled around them, and the sled moved like the wind. Kai was very frightened. He tried to say his prayers, but he could remember only his multiplication tables.

The snowflakes grew and grew until they looked like white hens running near them. At last the big sled stopped and the driver stood up. Kai knew her at once. She was the Snow Queen!

"How cold you look," she said. "Come closer and let me warm you." She put her cloak around Kai and kissed his forehead. Her kiss was like an icy wound, yet at once Kai felt stronger, and he did not notice how cold the air was. As he stared into the Snow Queen's face, he thought he had never seen anyone wiser or more beautiful. The longer he looked, the less he knew, and soon all memory of Gerda and the Grandmother vanished.

They set out again, and now they left the earth and were flying in the air. They circled back over his town, but Kai did not even see it. Above oceans, lakes, and mountains they flew, spurred by the wind. He could hear the cry of the wolves and the cawing of the crows. The white moon came out and traveled with them across the sky. When daytime came, Kai slept at the feet of the Snow Queen.

It was a sad, gray winter. As time passed, people in the town began to say that Kai must have drowned in the icy river that ran close to the square where the boys played with their sleds. But Gerda could not believe this.

One clear morning in early spring she put on her new red shoes and crept out of the house. Down to the river she went and threw her shoes into the water. "Is it true that you have taken Kai?" she asked the river. "Here are my new red shoes if you will give him back to me."

The shoes struck the water far from shore, but the river carried them back to her as if to say it had not taken Kai. Gerda did not understand. She thought she had not thrown the shoes far enough, so she climbed into a rowboat that was in the reeds and threw the shoes over the water again. Just then the boat drifted with the current, and Gerda found herself floating down the river.

"Perhaps it will carry me to where Kai is," thought Gerda, and she sat perfectly still in her stocking feet. The land along the shores was green and beautiful, and sparrows flew near the boat, chirping as if to comfort her. At last the boat drifted near a cherry orchard and came to rest upon the shore.

An old lady came out of a strange little house nearby and caught hold of the boat with her shepherd's crook. "You poor little thing," she said to Gerda. "Tell me who you are and how you have come to be here."

"I am searching for my playmate," said Gerda, and she told the old woman everything.

"You must not be sad. Your friend will probably pass this way soon. Come and eat my cherries and I will show you all the flowers in my garden." The old woman took Gerda by the hand and led her into the house. The windows were made of colored glass and a strange light shone in the room. On a table stood a silver bowl full of ripe cherries. As Gerda ate them and stayed with the woman, she thought of Kai less and less.

The old woman knew witchcraft, but she was not evil, and she had always wanted a little girl. That evening, when Gerda had fallen asleep, the woman went into the garden and pointed her shepherd's crook at the rose trees. At once they sank into the ground and disappeared. She was afraid that if Gerda saw the roses, she would think of Kai and run away.

In the morning she took the girl outside and showed her the garden. Gerda played in the golden sunshine with the flowers and came to know every one. But always something seemed to be missing, and she could not think what it was.

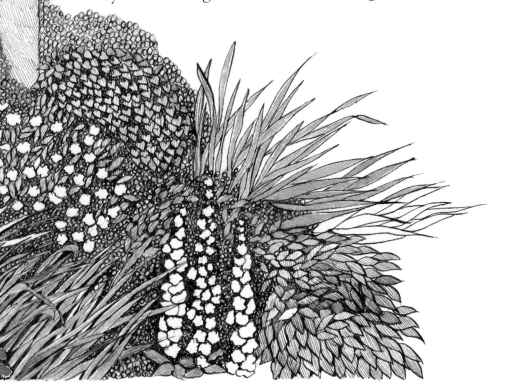

Many weeks passed and Gerda might have stayed forever, lulled by the old woman's kindness and the beauty of the place. But one day she noticed the painting of a rose on a broad-brimmed hat the woman often wore. At once she leaped up and ran outside. Why were there no roses among all the flowers in the garden? Gerda was so sad that she wept, and where her tears fell, a rose tree suddenly grew up. She breathed in the fragrance of the flowers and thought of the roses at home and of Kai.

"I have stayed here far too long!" she cried. "I must find Kai. Do you know where he is?" she asked the roses.

"He is not dead," they answered. "We have been down under the earth where the dead people are, and Kai was not there."

Gerda ran among the flowers, asking all of them if they had seen Kai. But though the flowers sang to her, they knew only the words to their own songs.

In despair Gerda ran from the garden and unlatched the door in the garden wall. Outside, the earth was cold and gray. Suddenly Gerda realized that it was late autumn. Back in the old woman's garden she had not seen the seasons change. There, it was always summer, and the flowers of every season bloomed at once.

"I have wasted so much time," thought Gerda. "I must not wait here any longer." She walked through fields and forests, though there was frost on the ground and her bare feet stung. The leaves on the trees had turned to yellow, and a cold autumn mist dripped down through their branches. How harsh and sad the world seemed!

Finally Gerda found herself in a dark forest. In the evening it began to snow. Then there was a whoosh of dark wings, and a large crow landed near her. "Caw, caw," he cried.

By this Gerda knew he was greeting her in a friendly way. "Do you know where my friend Kai is?" she asked him.

"Perhaps," said the crow slowly. "There is a castle not far from here and in it lives a princess. Recently she has taken a husband, a young man who is a stranger and is rumored to be afraid of nothing."

Gerda cried out in excitement. "That must be Kai!"

"Well, perhaps," the crow answered. "He is said to have long hair and bright, shining eyes. Many before him had tried to win the princess. But it was the stranger she wanted, because he was far cleverer than all the rest."

"Now I know it is Kai," said Gerda. "He is so clever that he can figure in fractions. Won't you take me to the castle, dear crow? I must see him at once."

The crow looked thoughtfully at Gerda, and then he nodded. "This way," he said. And he rose up into the air and flew ahead of her out of the forest.

As they entered the castle Gerda was nearly faint with longing. She was certain the bridegroom must be Kai. Soon she would see his face. He would smile at her and tell her how happy he was that she had found him at last.

Gerda followed the crow up the backstairs to the bridal chamber. The castle was dim and quiet. But suddenly there was a whirling, rushing sound, and shadows of horses and hunters, of dogs and falcons, moved upon the walls. Gerda drew back fearfully.

"Do not be afraid," said the crow. "They are only dreams come to fetch the princess and her bridegroom. They will be fast asleep, and you will learn if he is the one you seek."

At last they arrived in the royal bedchamber. Gerda peeked at the bride-groom where he lay and saw his long brown hair upon the pillow. "It is Kai!" she shouted with joy. Then the dreams rushed in again, and the young man awoke and looked her in the face.

But it was not Kai, not Kai at all!

With no thought for where she was, Gerda began to weep. "You poor thing," said the prince. "Tell us what is the matter."

As Gerda told them all that had happened, the princess held her close. They said she must spend the night, and in the morning when she awoke, they gave her a silk dress and a pair of boots and a coach drawn by four horses. For a time the crow rode with her. But when they came to the edge of the forest, he had to fly away. Gerda waved and waved until she could no longer see his wings shining in the distance. Now she was alone and felt sadder and more desolate than ever.

At length they came to a stand of trees along the roadside. Hidden among them was a band of robbers and the golden coach dazzled their eyes like a flame. "Gold! Gold!" they screamed, flinging themselves upon it. They grabbed hold of the horses and killed the coachman, and then they dragged Gerda out upon the road.

"She is lovely and plump," said an old robber woman. "I think I will have her for supper." She took a long knife from her belt, and her eyes sparkled with greed.

But just as the robber woman was about to slit poor Gerda's throat, her daughter, whom she was carrying upon her back, bit her hard. "No, she is mine. I want to play with her," said the little robber girl. She was a spoiled and willful child, and so the robbers had to give in.

Late that night when they arrived at the robbers' castle, the girl asked Gerda if she was a princess.

"No, I am not," answered Gerda, and then she told her how she was looking for Kai and had come to be riding in such a fine carriage.

The robber girl looked very seriously at her then and nodded. "I won't allow them to kill you even if I do get angry at you. I will do it myself."

Gerda was very frightened. The walls of the robbers' castle were black with smoke, and ravens flew in and out of the tower. Dogs roamed freely through the halls. They jumped up in the air but they did not bark; that was not permitted.

In the corner where the robber girl slept were all her pet animals. Two wood pigeons were kept in a cage high up in the rafters, and a reindeer stood tied near her bed. "I like to keep them imprisoned," she told Gerda. "It amuses me to see their sorrow."

The little robber girl went to sleep with her knife clutched in her hand, but Gerda was afraid to close her eyes. She did not know if she was going to live or die. In the middle of the night, suddenly one of the wood pigeons cooed. "We have seen Kai. He sat in the Snow Queen's sled and white hens ran near them. She has carried him to a land far to the north. You must ask the reindeer where it is. He will know."

"Oh, yes. Ice and snow are always there. It is a wonderful place," the reindeer said. "There an animal can roam freely in the shining valleys. That is where I was born." Then he grew silent, remembering all he had lost.

In the morning Gerda told the robber girl what she had heard from the animals. She listened quite solemnly and then she jumped out of bed and hugged Gerda. "I will help you. Leave me your pretty dress and your boots. You shall take the reindeer. He will carry you to your friend."

28

She tied Gerda onto the reindeer's back and gave her some meat and two loaves of bread. Away they went, as fast as they could, farther and farther north. They heard the wolves howl and the ravens call, and suddenly the sky was filled with great arcs of color. They were the northern lights.

At last they came to a little cottage at the border of Lapland. An old woman came out, and they told her where they were bound. "You must find my friend, the Finnish woman. She will be able to help you," the old woman said. She wrote a note on a piece of dried codfish, and they set out once more.

When they reached the Finnish woman's house, they had to knock on the chimney, for the door was nearly buried under the snow. But inside the house it was as hot as an oven. The Finnish woman gave the reindeer a piece of ice to cool his head and read three times what was written on the codfish.

Poor Gerda was so tired that she fell asleep in the corner. Then the reindeer and the Finnish woman talked together quietly. "You are very wise," the reindeer said. "Can't you make a magic drink so that Gerda will be able to defeat the Snow Queen?"

The woman smiled at him and patted his nose. "I can give her no more power than she has already. Don't you see how people and animals must serve her? Don't you see how she has been able to journey so far, though her feet are bare? No, my friend, Gerda's power is in her heart. Her goodness and innocence are the only weapons against the Snow Queen." She woke Gerda up then and lifted her onto the reindeer's back.

He ran a short way over the snowy earth and set her down beside a bush with red berries. It was at the edge of the Snow Queen's gardens. Gerda looked back at him only once and saw that his face was streaked with tears. Then she followed the path and ran toward the Snow Queen's palace as fast as she could.

Suddenly she saw hundreds of snowflakes. They whirled along just above the earth, growing larger as they came near. Some looked like huge porcupines, others like snakes writhing together; still others were like bears with cruel, grinning faces. All the snowflakes were blindingly white and horribly alive. They were the Snow Queen's army on the march.

Gerda stopped short. Her breath came fast, forming vapor in the frozen air. As she stood there it became more solid and shaped itself into a band of angels armed with shields and spears. They threw their spears at the snow creatures, shattering them into thousands of pieces. There were no more barriers after that, and Gerda was able to walk into the Snow Queen's palace.

The palace walls were glittering ice, and the windows and doors were made of wind. In the glare of the northern lights Gerda could see the gates opening before her. Echoing, vast, and cold was the Snow Queen's palace. Yet Gerda had come so far already and she was not afraid.

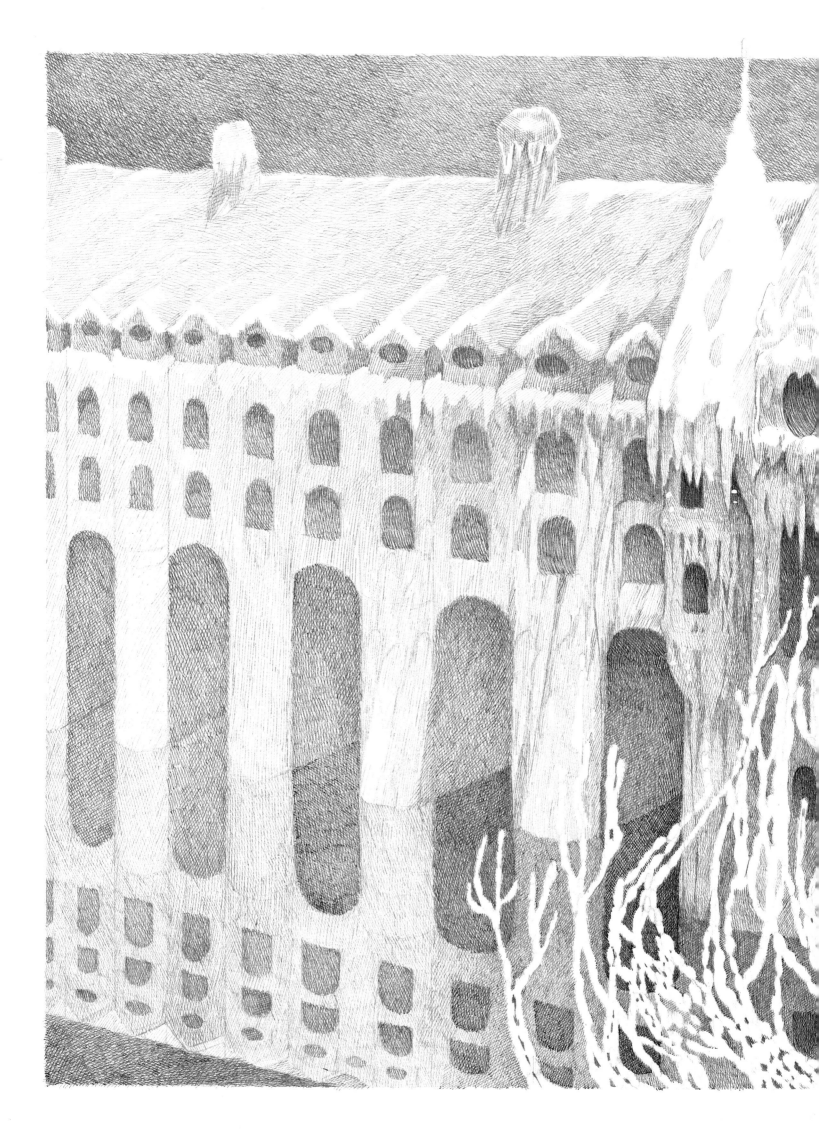

She ran through halls of drifted snow that turned and twisted for miles. At last she saw a tiny figure, blue with cold, seated on a frozen lake. As Gerda drew closer she saw that it was Kai. He was playing with pieces of ice, arranging them into patterns. The game was very important because the Snow Queen had promised that if he could form the right word she would give him the world and a new pair of skates. The word was *eternity*, but Kai could not remember it no matter how hard he tried.

He did not even look up when Gerda rushed at him and threw her arms around his poor, stiff body. She began to cry, and her hot tears fell upon his heart and melted the ice away. Only then could he see her.

"Gerda, oh, Gerda. Is it really you? Where have you been for so long? What place is this, Gerda? Why is it so cold and empty here?" As he looked around him Kai burst into tears. He wept and wept until the grains of glass in his eyes were washed away. Then he held on to Gerda as if he would never let her go.

So glad were they to be together that they never even noticed that the pieces of ice had formed themselves into the word Kai had been trying to make. Now the Snow Queen could return, and it would not matter, for Kai's right to freedom was written upon the frozen lake.

Then Gerda took his hand and they walked out of the Snow Queen's palace. They spoke of the Grandmother and of the roses that bloomed in the window gardens. The wind had died down and the sun shone through the clouds. At last they reached the bush where the reindeer was waiting. Now there was a younger one, too, whose udder was full of warm milk for them to drink. Kai and Gerda climbed upon the reindeers' backs and the animals carried them along until blades of grass started to break through the snow.

"Good-bye, good-bye," the children called. It was early spring. They heard birds singing and saw that the trees were all in bud. The towers of their own city were shining in the distance.

Soon they were walking up the stairs to the Grandmother's house. Nothing had changed. The clock on the wall was ticking and the wheels inside it moved. But when Kai and Gerda stepped through the doorway, they knew that they had grown up. They were no longer children.

In the window gardens they saw the roses blooming. There were the little stools they used to sit upon. As they went out into the sunshine all memory of the Snow Queen's palace and its empty splendor vanished. There they sat, the two of them, and it was summer, a beautiful summer day.